Cinnamon Lake Mysteries

Soup Kitchen Suspicion

Clear Creek Christian School

Dandi Daley Mackall
Illustrated by Kay Salem

CPH
SAINT LOUIS

To my dad, F. R. Daley, M.D., who helped me with this story. In his memory, this book is dedicated to his grandchildren: Kelly and Chris Pento, and Jenny, Katy, and Dan Mackall.

Copyright © 1998 Dandi Daley Mackall
Published by Concordia Publishing House
3558 S. Jefferson Avenue, St. Louis, MO 63118-3968
Manufactured in the United States of America

Library of Congress Cataloging-in-Publication Data

Mackall, Dandi Daley.
    Soup kitchen suspicion / Dandi Daley Mackall ; illustrated by Kay Salem.
        p. cm. -- (Cinnamon Lake mysteries ; 6)
    Summary: When they are asked to work in the church soup kitchen, Molly and the other Cinnamon Lakers are drawn into a mystery surrounding missing funds and they learn that appearances can sometimes be deceiving.
    ISBN 0-570-05312-9
[1. Clubs--Fiction. 2. Soup kitchens--Fiction. 3. Christian life--Fiction. 4. Mystery and detective stories.] I. Salem, Kay, ill. II. Title. III. Series.
PZ7.M1905Sr 1998
[FIC]--dc21
                                        97-30163
                                           AC

1 2 3 4 5 6 7 8 9 10   07 06 05 04 03 02 01 00 99 98

Cinnamon Lake Mysteries

*I'm not sure how we got famous
as the Cinnamon Lake Mystery Club.
I mean, the Cinnamon Lake part
is easy. That's where we live.
The mystery part is more ...
mysterious.*

Contents

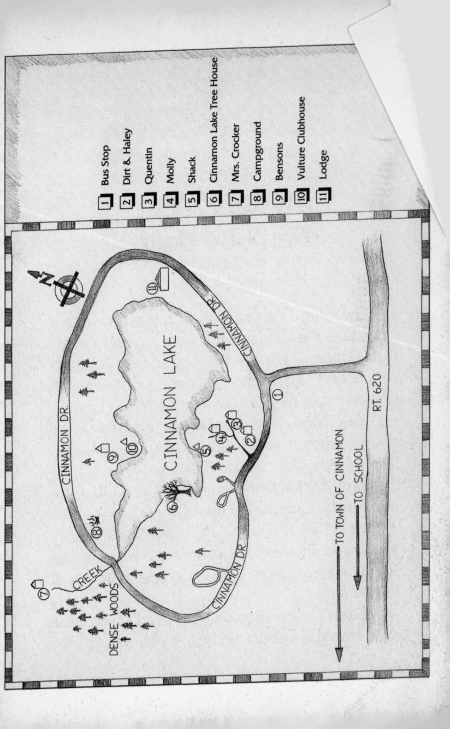

1. Bus Stop
2. Dirt & Haley
3. Quentin
4. Molly
5. Shack
6. Cinnamon Lake Tree House
7. Mrs. Crocker
8. Campground
9. Bensons
10. Vulture Clubhouse
11. Lodge

CINNAMON LAKE

CINNAMON DR.

DENSE WOODS

CREEK

N

TO TOWN OF CINNAMON

TO SCHOOL

RT. 620

1

Mystery Meat
Can't Be Beat

"Quentin, I can't stand it. It's our first *real* case! Like the Cinnamon Lakers are real detectives, I mean." He was moving so fast, I tripped on packed snow trying to keep up. We were only a couple blocks from Granny Mae's church.

"Yes, Molly. So you've stated at least a dozen times now." His hoarse voice came in frost clouds, like cartoon bubbles.

"Didn't your grandmother tell you what the mystery is, Quentin?" I asked.

"I told you, Molly," he said. "She simply requested we meet her at the soup kitchen. She has a mystery for the Cinnamon Lakers. That's all I know."

I hadn't even known Quentin's Granny Mae was starting a soup kitchen. Even though we walked fast, I shivered with the icy cold of February. "It's not like we've never solved a mystery," I said. "But this is like being hired. Of course we'd never charge Granny Mae."

"From what my mother says, Granny could never pay anyway. She spent her savings to get this food program for the poor underway. An unsound investment," Quentin said.

I recognized the church just ahead. "Quentin, do you think anybody will see us go in?" I hoped they wouldn't mistake us for the needy people who would probably show up at the soup kitchen. I knew I shouldn't think like that. But lately, I couldn't help it.

"Precisely whom do you fear, Molly Mack? That fellow there?" Quentin pointed at a shabby-looking, bald man leaning against the church. He wore no stocking cap, and I could see holes in his coat.

The man frowned. His beady eyes sent a different kind of chill down my back. I'd seen him around before. Once he'd yelled at me when he stepped in front of my bike. I'd wiped out trying to get out of his way.

We'd reached the back door of Granny Mae's church. I took a quick look around and stepped inside.

"Hmm," Quentin said. "Wonder what Trevor's doing here."

"No! Where?" I pulled off my stocking cap and fluffed up my hair.

Quentin muffled a laugh. "I guess I was mistaken." And he stepped down the stairs ahead of me.

As cold as I'd been, I felt my face heat up. Quentin knew. But how could he? Quentin never notices anything. Especially crushes. He's too busy doing his scientific experiments.

Trevor. I even liked the sound of his name. Last week he had shown up at school. Just appeared—like a prince from a faraway country. Turned out he's the mayor's son. He'd been living with his mother in California. *Trevor.*

Valentine's Day was three days away. Only Trevor didn't know I was alive.

A whiff of garlic brought me back. Granny Mae's laugh rolled up from the basement. "Girlfriend, put that in here with the meat!" More laughter.

Four long tables crossed the basement. The cold, concrete floor sloped toward the kitchen. Quentin already had his hand sunk into a bowl of potato chips.

"Molly Mack," Quentin's Granny Mae said,

"wash your hands. Then I'll tell you where to get them work-dirty."

"Okay, Granny Mae," I said. "But what about the case?"

She shook her head and gave me a shush look. I figured this must be a *real* mystery. She didn't even want the other helpers to know about it.

"Hey, Sunny!" I called. Sunny's the rich Cinnamon Laker. I hoped I looked half as out of place in the soup kitchen as she did in her expensive red pants and flowered sweater. She waved but kept studying the pot Granny was stirring.

"Smells like *kimchi*," she said.

"What's *kimchi?*" Granny asked.

"It's a Korean specialty. You put everything you've got in a pot and cook it."

"I'll be," Granny said. "That's *my* recipe. But I call it mystery meat."

Granny's friend the librarian was filling ice cube trays. A white-haired lady stood over a sink of soap suds. A younger woman, carrying a big box, stumbled out of a closet. "These the cups you wanted, Mae?" she asked. "Have you read what's on them?"

"I don't think our guests are going to care what's written on their drink cups," said Granny

Mae. "Molly, how'd you like to be in charge of drinks?"

"Sure," I said. But I didn't want to be in charge of anything. I wanted to know about the mystery.

As soon as they handed me the cups, I recognized them. We still had tons of them at our house. My dad works for an advertising company. He can come up with a slogan for anything. It's not *his* fault if the company messes it up. The paper cups read: *Thin Drink!* It was supposed to say, "Thin*k* Drink!" The printer forgot the *k*.

Quentin peered over my shoulder. "Good," he said. "I was afraid they might be the cups your father designed for the new gas station."

"That wasn't his fault," I said. "*We'll fill you fast and cheap!* was a great slogan."

"Yes," Quentin admitted. "But they were not bound to attract many customers with *We'll **KILL** you fast and cheap.*" Quentin sighed. "What a difference a letter makes."

Granny kept us all hopping. I'd almost forgotten about our mystery when I heard someone go, "*Pssst.*" I turned to see Granny Mae crooking her finger at me. Soon as I spotted her, she disappeared into the supply closet. I elbowed Quentin and tugged Sunny to follow me.

Granny was waiting for us. We stepped into the closet. Granny shut the door after us. Then she yanked a string that turned on the overhead lightbulb. Reaching into her apron pocket, Granny produced a wrinkly piece of paper. It looked like old parchment, the kind they wrote the Declaration of Independence on. The crinkly, brown paper had been rolled up like a scroll.

Granny carefully untied the piece of string from around the scroll. "There wouldn't be a soup kitchen if it hadn't been for what I'm about to show you," she said.

She handed me the scroll. I unrolled it and stared at the words:

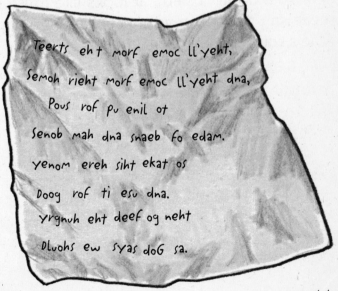

Teerts eht morf emoc ll'yeht,
Semoh rieht morf emoc ll'yeht dna,
Pous rof pu enil ot
Senob mah dna snaeb fo edam.
yenom ereh siht ekat os
Doog rof ti esu dna.
yrgnuh eht deef og neht
Dluohs ew syas doG sa.

"What's it mean?" Sunny asked.

"Maybe it's a foreign language," I said. "Wasn't the Bible written in Hebrew? Maybe that's what it is."

Granny whispered, "Somebody left this note at church in an envelope with my name on it. And inside that envelope ... $300. I'd like to know what the note says. And I'm counting on the Cinnamon Lakers to find the generous soul who made this soup kitchen possible. Find them before Saturday. I want to say thank you at my Valentine's dinner at the soup kitchen. But keep your investigations secret until we know who it is."

"We'll do it!" I said. "It looks like mystery meat isn't the only mystery cooking in Granny Mae's soup kitchen."

2

Just in Time
A Coded Rhyme

"It's not Korean or any language I've seen," Sunny said, taking the note from me.

"It looks like Martian language might look, don't you think?" I said.

Quentin snatched the note out of Sunny's hands. "Mere speculations. I shall crack this code in no time."

"And, Grandson," Granny Mae said, throwing open the closet door, "I shall crack the whip. We still have a dinner to put on." She shooshed us out of the closet.

"Hey! Some soup kitchen. Where's the soup?"

"I'm sorry, little girl," said the white-haired lady. "We aren't ready to serve yet. Please wait until we open the side door around ..."

"Dirt!" I said, coming to the rescue. "It's okay, ma'am. She's with us."

Dirt Harrison is going to be an archaeologist when she grows up. That's a person who digs in the ground for old stuff. Dirt digs in the dirt a lot. She's the toughest first-grader in the world. Probably the toughest Cinnamon Laker, even though the rest of us are at least two years older.

Dirt was wearing baggy jeans and army boots. Her raggy, gray sweatshirt had tape splotches where letters had rubbed almost off. I could understand how somebody took her for one of the eaters instead of the servers.

Sunny brushed the snow off Dirt's wild, wind-blown hair. "Hi, Dirt," she said.

Dirt shook her head to mess up her hair again. "So?" she asked. "Who took the soup?"

"There isn't any soup," Sunny answered. "We're serving mystery meat." She ran off to help with the salad.

Dirt turned to me. "Far out. Then why do they call it a soup kitchen?"

I looked around for help. Granny Mae shrugged.

"Yuck!" came a whine from the stairwell. "What's that awful smell? I don't see any poor and needy. Who chose the paint for these walls, anyway?"

Quentin and I looked at each other across the kitchen. At the same time, we said, "Haley's here."

Sure enough, there was Haley Harrison. She's in third grade, like Quentin and Sunny and me. Haley's pink tights and skirt stuck out from her ski parka. It's hard to believe she and Dirt are sisters. Haley looks like part of a doll collection. If they didn't already have fashion dolls, they'd probably make Haley dolls.

Haley pranced softly on the cement, never taking her gaze from the floor. "I'm here," Haley announced. "I said I'd come, and I came."

So all the Cinnamon Lakers had made it. Our club, the Cinnamon Lakers, meets in a tree by the lake. But not when it's freezing February. Mostly we try to do good stuff. Since Jesus has done so much for us, especially by dying on the cross for us, we figure the least we can do is try to help other people.

Quentin popped what looked like an olive into his mouth. "Actually," he said, "this food is quite acceptable. Except for the pies."

"My mother baked those pies," Haley said.

Quentin paid no attention. He whipped out

a pencil from behind his ear and scribbled something on the mystery note. I started to fill Dirt and Haley in on our case, but Granny interrupted.

"Are you Cinnamon Lakers going to stand around flapping your jaws all day?" Granny Mae asked. She gave us all orders. Dirt and I got to work on the drinks. I made orange drink in a silver pitcher. The pitcher sounded like a gong every time I stirred the drink. Dirt put cold water in another pitcher. We stuck them in the frig and tried to figure out the coffeepot.

Granny Mae hollered above all the kitchen noise: " 'Whoever wants to become great among you must be your servant.' Matthew 20:26. So get to serving. Amen!"

Granny's friend shouted *Amen!* back.

After a minute, Sunny asked, "Granny Mae, are there really poor people in Cinnamon? I don't think I've ever known a really poor person."

Sunny didn't say it snotty. She probably *hadn't* seen anybody poor. Her dad's a land developer who travels around getting rich. She lives out in Cinnamon Lake where I live, a couple of miles from Cinnamon.

"Nah," said Haley. "I've lived here my whole

16

life and never tripped over a homeless person—
not even on this end of town. I think the people
who will come are freeloaders. Just here for free
food. Like Quentin."

We all looked where Haley was pointing.
Quentin was in the act of stuffing two chocolate
chip cookies in his mouth.

"Honey," Granny Mae said, "there's not a
town on God's good earth, but there's a corner
in it with God's own poor. Everybody has trou-
bles sometimes."

"We have precisely 17 minutes left,"
Quentin said, wiping crumbs from his chin. "In 6
minutes, the meat will be browned. At that
time, we shall transfer said meat into the serving cooker. One and one-half minutes. At 7
minutes to, salad people get set. Plastic wrap in
place for 6 more minutes. Beverage pitchers
may be set out at that time."

Quentin inspected the coffeepot. "Perking,"
he announced. "Orange drink?"

"Refrigerator," I answered. I felt like I should
say "sir."

"Water?" Quentin barked.

"Faucet," Dirt answered.

Quentin frowned. He looked from his watch
to the mystery note.

"That's my boy," Granny Mae said, shaking her head.

"How many places should I set, Granny?" Sunny asked.

"I think 30 ought to do it. We might grow once word gets out."

I couldn't see how we'd pull this off. Every few minutes I checked on Quentin to see how he was coming with the code. I could almost hear his gray cells whirring. That's what Quentin calls thinking—using his gray cells.

We fell to working so hard I couldn't believe it when Quentin hollered his warning: "Two minutes!"

There was no way we could be ready to feed 30 people in two minutes. I caught Granny Mae's eye. She pointed to heaven with one hand and stirred mystery meat with the other. I knew she meant to pray. I prayed.

We moved fast. A minute-and-a-half later Sunny had dropped a plate of pickles, Haley had broken a fingernail, and I'd spilled potato chips all over the floor.

"Take your places on the line!" yelled Granny. It was like being backstage on opening night.

Everybody put on plastic gloves like the

school cafeteria ladies wear. Granny stood behind a pot full of mystery meat. I stood next to her with the buns. Then Haley with chips, Sunny with salad, and finally Dirt, who guarded the drinks.

Quentin started a 30-second countdown. "30 ... 29 ..." He stopped. He pulled the mystery note out of his pocket, shook it, and held it up. "It's backward!" he shouted. Quentin scribbled on the note, wadded it, and tossed it to me. It almost landed in the mystery meat. "10 ... 9 ..." Quentin said, picking up his countdown.

I smoothed out the scroll and read what Quentin had decoded. When you copied the words backward, it said:

They'll come from the street,
And they'll come from their homes,
To line up for soup
Made of beans and ham bones.
So take this here money and use it for good.
Then go feed the hungry as God says we should.

"Way to go, Quentin," I hollered to him.

But Quentin had one arm straight up and both eyes on his watch as he kept up his countdown. "3 ... 2 ... 1! Open the doors!"

3

Masses and Messes
Blue Jeans and Dresses

They kept coming. And coming. And coming!

"Oh, Lord," I heard Granny Mae say, "bless these fishes! And multiply our mystery meat."

"Molly, take over the meat," she said. She walked out to greet the crowd.

Quentin ran up and elbowed me. "Molly, look," he whispered. He nodded toward the first man in line. It was the scruffy man we'd seen outside. In the light I saw he had more hair on his face than on his head. His eyebrows were lowered in a permanent scowl.

"I'm Granny Mae. Welcome to the Lord's kitchen." She stuck out her hand. But the man didn't stick his out in return. So Granny just wiped her hand on her apron.

"The name's Budd," the man said.

"Glad to meet you, Mr. Budd," said Granny.

I was trying to figure out the meat scooper without dropping the buns. "Quentin, help," I begged.

Quentin pulled on a pair of plastic gloves. "All right, Molly," he said. "You need a system. I'll do buns. You scoop meat."

Mr. Budd held out his plate. His glare made me look away. Quentin reached over and plopped a bun on his plate.

"Well?" Mr. Budd said.

I scooped up mystery meat and emptied it onto his plate. I aimed for the bun, but my hand shook. It was my first try. I missed. Mystery meat spread all over his plate—everywhere except on the bun. "Sorry," I said, showing him my winning smile.

"Kids," he grumbled. He moved down the line. I heard him bark at Dirt, "Where's the hot tea? I hate coffee."

Everybody else coming through the line was nice. A little boy smiled at me and said, "Thank you, ma'am."

One woman said, "I think it's wonderful what you kids are doing to help. God bless you." Nobody was grumpy. Nobody except Mr. Budd. And I hoped he wouldn't come back for seconds.

"And who are you?"

I looked up from my mystery meat to see a tall gentleman. That's the first thing I thought when I saw him. Hat in hand, a white handkerchief folded neatly in the pocket of his shiny, brown striped suit. A gentleman.

"Such a lovely lady to serve me a lovely dinner," he said. "Now this is certainly more than I might have anticipated. Her beauty is as a rose, more delicate and fairer still."

Me? A lovely lady? A rose? I felt my face turn rose-red. "I'm Molly Mack," I said. I started to shake his hand. Then I remembered my plastic gloves.

"A comely name for a charming girl," he said. He bowed, sweeping his hat in front of him.

"Serve him, Molly," Quentin commanded. "They're still coming in."

"Your learned friend is absolutely correct. No doubt the brains behind your organization," said the gentleman. "Mr. Roosevelt, sir," he said to Quentin. "Most pleased to make your acquaintance."

I could tell Quentin didn't quite know what to say. He nodded. Mr. Roosevelt moved down the line. I kept scooping.

A beautiful African American girl came through. Probably a teenager. "Is this an international kitchen?" she asked.

"Huh?" I said.

"I mean, you seem to be multicultural." She had a perfect smile.

I looked down our line. She was right. There was me—Irish. Quentin, Granny Mae, and her friend were African American. Then Sunny—Korean. Baby doll Haley. And Dirt, who might have come from another planet.

The mystery meat was getting low. All the chairs filled up. Some people stood to eat. And still more people came.

Granny whizzed by. "I've called for more troops," she said. "In the meantime, make those scoops smaller. More mystery—less meat."

Mystery! As we scooped, I considered how we could track down Granny's mystery millionaire. Interviews? Fingerprints? Phone …

"You call that *hot*?"

The gruff voice behind me made me jump. The full scoop of mystery meat plopped all over me. I looked up to see the frowning Mr. Budd.

He eyed me up and down. Then he shook his head and walked away—leaving me covered with brown blobs.

"Allow me to assist." It was the gentleman, Mr. Roosevelt. "I couldn't help noticing your difficulty." He took the scoop from me. "I would be happy to stand in your place so you may retire and clean yourself up a bit."

I thanked him. And I hoped Mr. Budd would be gone when I got back. I spun around to head for the washroom before anybody else saw me. And *smack!* I ran right into somebody.

"Excuse me," I stammered. "I was ..." I looked up into the biggest pair of blue eyes. *Gulp!* "Trevor?"

4

Have a Vulture Interview Here Comes Mystery Number Two!

Trevor stared at me, his nose scrunched up. Like he'd smelled something awful. Like he'd seen something awful. *Me.*

I ran away. Ducking my head, I flew past the stairwell to the washroom before Trevor could say anything. Before anybody else saw me. But I wasn't quick enough.

"Molly Mack! Aren't you looking stunning!"

It was Ben Benson, followed by his little brother, Sam. Bringing up the rear was Marty, Quentin's cousin. *Vultures!* They have a club on the other side of the lake from the Cinnamon Lakers' tree house. *Vultures* is the perfect name for them. Vultures feed on living creatures.

Marty, Ben, Sam, and their buddies feed on us. Everything we try to do, they try even harder to mess up.

"Nice outfit, Mack," Marty said. "Are they giving out free clothes to the poor too?" Then he cackled. He was chewing on aluminum foil. In the dark of the stairwell, sparks flew out of his mouth.

"What are you doing here?" I demanded, brushing mystery meat from my neck and hair.

"My grandmother drives a hard bargain," Marty said. "We're her extra troops. And is she ever going to owe me big time for this one."

"I thought you told me you had to come because Granny Mae threatened to tell your mom on us if you didn't," Ben said.

If looks could kill, Ben would have dropped dead from the glare Marty shot him. Ben and Marty are fifth-graders who look like high school thugs, if you ask me. Sam Benson, Ben's brother, is in third grade. Sometimes he's not so bad. Except when he's around Ben and Marty.

"From the looks of you, Molly," Sam said, "this joint needs our help. Vultures rule!" Sam charged off toward the kitchen.

Didn't Granny Mae have enough mystery— enough trouble? Did she have to invite Vultures into her soup kitchen?

I escaped to the washroom and got most of the junk off my sweatshirt. I told myself I had a job to do. A mystery to solve. I tried to focus. Who had given money to Granny Mae? Where did the note come from? We had to start interviewing suspects right away. I'd just have to do my best to keep away from Vultures ... and from Trevor.

Staying away from Trevor turned out to be easy. When I got back to the kitchen, he was already gone. "Mr. Roosevelt?" I asked, taking over my scooping job. "Did you see a nice-looking, blond boy with big blue eyes come through here?"

"He came, he saw, he left," said Mr. Roosevelt. He smiled gently at me. "And parting is such sweet sorrow."

I wasn't sure what he meant. But I liked him. His shiny, striped suit made him look like an actor on the stage. Or on public television. He even had an English accent like Shakespeare.

Finally, the crowd thinned. Our serving line closed, just as I spooned out the last drops of mystery meat. I spotted the librarian resting in a folding chair off in the corner. The perfect choice for my first interview.

"Big crowd, eh, Mrs. Donnelson," I said, pulling up a chair beside her. I remembered Granny's warning to keep our investigations secret until we had our answer.

"There must have been 75 people, Molly. Maybe more. I don't know how we fed them all." She had her legs stretched out, crossed at the ankles. She'd kicked off one shoe, and it hung from her big toe. Those shoes looked awfully expensive to me. But I wasn't sure how much money librarians made.

"So, Mrs. Donnelson," I said, stretching my legs out like hers, crossing my ankles, "I was thinking about becoming a librarian when I grow up. Is there a lot of money in it?"

The librarian broke out laughing. "I wouldn't get into it for the money, if I were you, Molly," she said. "You can make a living, but that's all."

I could check that one out, I supposed. "Hmmm, so you don't have a lot left over, say ... for helping the homeless? And stuff like that?" I added quickly.

Mrs. Donnelson sat up straight, tilted her head, and squinted at me. "If you're trying to ask me to donate to Granny's soup kitchen, I would if I could, dear. I do what I can. That's why I'm helping out this way." She got up and carried empty dishes to the kitchen.

I grabbed a napkin and started a list of suspects on it. First, I wrote *Mrs. Donnelson.* Then I crossed out her name. I looked around the room. Then I wrote down the names of the other two grown-ups who'd helped serve. It was a start.

Little by little, the eaters left. A few men sat on the stairs, drinking coffee. A couple of them started to smoke. Granny asked them to go outside. We all pitched in to clean up. Dirt swept the floor. Sunny and Haley—mostly Sunny—washed dishes. I dried dishes and put them away.

Ben and Marty were goofing off, playing football with Sam's stocking cap.

"You boys can set the table for tomorrow," Granny said firmly.

They groaned, but even Vultures are no match for Granny Mae. Marty barked orders. Sam and Ben struggled with a roll of white paper we used for tablecloths.

About a half hour later, Ben yelled out, "This has got to come from Molly!" He was cracking up so much, he could hardly get the words out. Sam held up one of Dad's *Thin Drink* cups.

"Didn't I ask you boys to set the table?"

Granny asked.

"We did!" Marty whined back.

"Do you expect us to eat with our fingers?" Granny asked. "Silverware, please."

"We couldn't find it," Marty said.

"Honestly." Granny Mae threw her dish towel over her shoulder and stormed to the kitchen. "It's right in this dr—" She didn't finish.

I kept my eyes on Marty. But I heard Granny Mae in the kitchen. She opened drawers. She slammed cupboards. I ran to see what was going on. "What's the matter, Granny Mae?" I asked.

She stared at me, her eyes wide. "It's gone!" she cried.

"No way," I said. "I dried the silverware and put it right in here." I pulled the silverware drawer open. It was empty! I stuck my hand inside all the way to the back. Nothing.

"It's not here!" I said, leaning against the drawer for support. "Somebody stole the silverware!"

5

Star Light, Star Bright
Something's Not Right

We spread out in Granny's soup kitchen and searched for the silverware. But it was no use. Every knife, fork, and spoon was gone.

"Looks like the ol' dish ran away with the spoon, huh," Sam said, yawning.

"We have to get going, Granny," Marty said. "Vulture business."

Granny mumbled thanks for coming. Quentin and I watched as Marty, Ben, and Sam disappeared up the basement stairs. "Are your little gray cells thinking what my little gray cells are thinking?" I asked.

"No doubt my gray cells produced the idea first," he said. "But I checked their pockets. They are not carrying the stolen silverware."

I wasn't ready to give up on Marty and Ben so fast. I only hoped Sam wasn't in on it.

Suddenly, Dirt popped out from under the sink. "Not there," she said, rubbing her hands together. The kid was grungy from head to foot. "I say we nail the Vultures on this one."

Sunny joined us. "This is so exciting!" she said. "Two mysteries for the price of one. Do you think the Vultures did it?"

"Quentin says no. Their pockets were empty," I said.

"Molly, you must never misquote me. I said their pockets did not contain the silverware. They may indeed be guilty. They may have an accomplice who sneaked out with the silverware before we noticed."

"Far out," Dirt said. "I'll search the Vulture clubhouse at midnight."

"Dirt," I said, "you shouldn't be out searching for silverware at midnight."

"It's cool," Dirt said. "I've got owls near there."

"You've got what?" I asked. But I knew that was all I'd get from her. Dirt was self-appointed caretaker of all kinds of creatures at Cinnamon Lake. She'd been known to raise orphan bats, nurse fallen woodpeckers, help hatch wren eggs, and single-handedly save a family of chip-munks.

"Tomorrow night we'll establish shifts to keep watch over all Vultures in Granny's kitchen," Quentin said. "Meanwhile, I'll get to work analyzing the note from our first mystery."

I handed the note over to Quentin. "What will you do with it, Quentin?"

He carefully rerolled the scroll. "I shall begin with a series of heat-sensitive experiments. Depending on my findings, I shall then apply …"

"That's okay," I said. I was too tired to hear the scientific details.

The librarian and Granny's other friend were putting on their coats. I heard them talking low: "I don't see how she'll make it to Saturday and her Valentine's dinner. Can you picture the mayor and all those businesspeople even coming here if word gets out about this?"

"Poor Mae," said the librarian. "Those church deacons took a lot of convincing to get her this trial week. She can kiss her Valentine's dinner good-bye." They walked upstairs, still whispering.

Haley came over and slipped into her pink ski jacket. "If you ask me, one of those poor people is not so poor tonight."

A horn honked. "Dirt!" Haley called. "That's

Mother. It's time to go."

"Go yourself," Dirt called. She was on her hands and knees behind the refrigerator. "I'll walk."

"No, not at this hour," Granny Mae said, pulling her out. "You go on now. You too, Sunny. And you go on too, Molly. I'll drive Quentin."

We put on our coats in silence. I hung back so I could talk to Granny Mae alone. "What will you do, Granny?"

"I'll replace that silver before the church ladies get all upset. I've got enough money from that anonymous giver." She put her arm around my shoulder and walked me upstairs and outside. We stood for a minute, looking up at a million stars. The only other light came from Mrs. H's car as Haley and Dirt climbed over each other getting in.

"But how will you get food to feed the people who come tomorrow?" I asked.

Granny smiled up at the stars. " 'Lift your eyes and look to the heavens: Who created all these? He who brings out the starry host one by one, and calls them each by name. Because of His great power and mighty strength, not one of them is missing.' Isaiah 40:26." Granny squeezed my shoulder then turned and walked away.

The horn honked again. Out the car window came Haley's whine. "Molly!"

On the ride back to Cinnamon Lake, I stared out the window at the stars. Too many to count. I knew Granny Mae was right. Not one of them was missing.

But the silver *was* missing. And Valentine's Day—my most hated day of the year—was just around the corner. Trevor didn't know I was alive. And Granny's soup kitchen was in big trouble. I remembered Granny telling me to lift my eyes to heaven. *God,* I prayed, *help me solve the mystery. Make that mysteries.*

The mystery meat was all gone. But what remained in Granny Mae's soup kitchen were two of the toughest mysteries the Cinnamon Lakers had ever faced. Who had given? And who had taken away?

6

Vultures Come,
Vultures Go
Maybe Yes, Maybe No

"We'll set a trap for the Vultures." I kept my voice down. Eric the Red and Bird, part-time Vultures, ruled the back of this bus. I'd called an emergency Cinnamon Lakers meeting for the next day after school. It was way too cold for our tree house, which was still all tree and no house. So we huddled at the front of bus number 4, the one that went to West Side Cinnamon by Granny's church.

"I told you the Vulture clubhouse was clean," Dirt said.

"Clean?" Haley asked.

"No hot goods," Dirt explained. "No stolen silverware. Get it now?"

"I'll tell Mother you were roaming the woods at midnight again," Haley said. "Not that she'd care. No-o-o. Dirt can do anything she wants. It's not fair. I …" She stopped in mid-sentence and looked around the bus. "Where's Sunny?"

"She plans to rendezvous with us at the soup kitchen," Quentin said. "I don't believe her father approves of this method of public transportation."

"Well, that's not fair," Haley whined. "If I have to ride the bus, I don't see why *Sunny* doesn't. Besides, are you even sure Granny Mae hasn't quit after last night?"

"She doesn't quit," Quentin said. "I admit I have wondered whether there would be ample food this time."

"I'll bet you have," Haley said.

"Could we please get back to our trap?" I said in a loud whisper. "I think we all agree Ben and Marty are still our prime suspects in mystery number 2." I flipped open my detective's notebook. Under *Mystery #2,* I had two names: *Marty* and *Ben.* "Since they didn't leave with the goods, and they didn't hide it in the clubhouse, the silverware may still be hidden somewhere in the church. We'll watch Ben and Marty and see if they lead us to it."

"And add Sam Benson to the list too," Haley said. "He'd steal just to get on Ben and Marty's good side."

"What good side?" Dirt said.

I added Sam to the list of suspects. "Okay. Tonight, it's Vulture watch. No matter how busy we are, we can't let them out of our sight."

"I have worked up a simple system of surveillance," Quentin said. "That means I have figured out a way to take turns watching any and all Vultures." Quentin showed us his plan. He had it worked out to the exact second. We'd take turns and trade off between suspects.

"I have made copies of the duty list." He handed us each a piece of paper with individual watch times to the minute.

"Last stop, children," called the bus driver.

We stared at each other. "Already?" I asked. Mr. Winkle, our bus driver, usually takes much longer. On this bus, I hadn't bounced off the seat once. And the bus driver hadn't yelled. The bus door hissed open, and cold air rushed in. We stepped to the curb. Not even one wheel of this bus was over the curb.

"I miss Mr. Winkle," Dirt said, pushing past us.

I'd been thinking about all the trouble Granny might be in by now. So it surprised me when I heard singing coming from the church basement.

We headed straight for the kitchen. Quentin frowned at his grandmother. "There is no sense pretending," he said. "My mother told me it took every last dollar to replace the stainless steel. Unless I have my facts out of order, there is nothing to be singing about."

"Then your facts are way out of order," Granny said.

I wanted to believe Granny. I pulled open the silverware drawer. "Granny, it's still empty!" I cried.

"Not to worry. They didn't have the right kind in the store," she said. "But they promised to have it here before supper."

"*Humph,*" said Quentin. "What about food?"

"Grandson, you just take your *humph* and open this refrigerator."

The silver refrigerator was four times the size of ours. Quentin grabbed one huge door. I took the other. We pulled.

"Noodles? Salad? Cheese? Casseroles?" Quentin said, his hoarse voice cracking.

I stared at boxes and bags and plates loaded

with food. "But where … who …?" I wondered if the Mystery Giver had struck again.

"Merchants, grocers," said Granny. "They'd have thrown most of it away. We only took what we'd eat ourselves though. The bags of lettuce have yesterday's date, but the salad's fine."

"Thrown it … away?" Quentin swallowed hard.

"And chocolate cake for dessert! What do you think of that?" It was the voice with the English accent.

"Mr. Roosevelt?" I asked, surprised to see him wearing Granny Mae's apron. "What are you doing here?"

"A fair question from a fair lady," he said. "Granny Mae has asked for my assistance. In exchange, she has graciously given me a warm place to spend the night."

"You call this hot?" Mr. Budd, wearing the exact same shirt as last night, cast a grumpy shadow over the kitchen. "This casserole tastes like dog food." He scribbled notes on a pad—in red ink, no less.

Mr. Roosevelt leaned down and whispered to me. "Mr. Budd's never-ending gripe list. He is my roommate for the week."

40

I kept my mouth shut. What I was thinking was *poor Mr. Roosevelt.* "But he lives in Cinnamon, doesn't he?"

"It would appear he lives in a poorly heated home. Or perhaps he wishes to save on heating costs. At least that's what he told the lovely Grandmother Mae."

That sounded funny to me. But I didn't have time to think about it. Ben Benson came thudding down the stairs. I checked my watch and Quentin's list. It was Dirt's shift. I saw her slide behind one of the coats and guessed she was peeking through the sleeve.

"Sammy's in trouble and can't come. Marty's just not coming. He made me come in his place. But I'm not staying all night," Ben said.

"And we're glad to have you," Granny said. "Right this way, Ben," she said, leading toward the sink. Dirt moved too.

Getting dinner out was a whole lot easier than the night before. Everything was already cooked. We just warmed stuff up or mixed it together. Fettuccine Alfredo, Mr. Roosevelt called it. Big pots of noodles in gooey sauce.

Sunny showed up and jumped right to work. The Cinnamon Lakers took shifts watching Ben.

During my shift, I saw him put three cookies in his pockets, but no silverware.

With 20 minutes to dinnertime, I found Granny in the supply closet. "Silverware come?" I asked.

"I'm sure it will be here any minute." She didn't look so sure. "I suppose I could have gotten plastic forks for backup. But that would have cost us a pretty penny. And besides, the manager himself promised me delivery."

The phone rang. Granny Mae raced to answer it. "That should be the silverware delivery boy asking directions."

"He better hurry," said Quentin. "In 15 minutes we open the doors."

"But you promised!" Granny's shout poured out of the kitchen. The rest of us stopped talking. "Can't you pick them up?" she begged the phone. Pause. "But that will be too late." That was the last thing she said. She stared at the telephone, then hung up, a blank look on her face.

The librarian spoke first. "Mae, now what?"

"I'll tell you now what," said Ben Benson. He turned from the stairwell, where he'd been staring up. From his smirk, I knew Ben was enjoying this. "That silverware ain't nothing. Wait till you see who's coming."

Granny ran to the bottom of the stairs. The rest of us watched her. Her whole body seemed to go stiff. "Why ... uh ... welcome to Granny Mae's soup kitchen," she said, "Mayor."

Mayor? Then that meant ... The mayor of Cinnamon stepped into the dining room. And right beside him, waiting to check out the food, was *Trevor.*

7

Chop, Chop
Please, Stop!

"Mayor," Quentin said. I had to hand it to him for trying to bail out his grandmother. "To what do we owe the honor of Your Honor's presence? We were not anticipating your arrival until Valentine's Day."

The mayor of Cinnamon's wide-eyed gaze darted into every corner of Granny Mae's soup kitchen. "Trevor … uh … raised some questions about your operation here. And as we were in the neighborhood, we decided to drop by."

Right, I thought. Trevor and his dad wouldn't be caught dead in this neighborhood unless they came to check it out. Why hadn't I curled my hair, just in case? I could have worn a different sweater.

Ben Benson stood smirking. "Hey, Trevor," he said.

Trevor walked off with Ben. Then he called over his shoulder, "Dad, Ben says they open the doors in 10 minutes. Then we're out of here. You promised."

"Ten minutes?" Granny Mae repeated. I could almost see her gray cells turning over in her head. I knew she was thinking what I was thinking. How were we going to serve fettuccine Alfredo with no silverware? "Mayor," she said, "I should tell you. We've got a prob—"

Dirt threw herself between Granny and the mayor. "Granny means we gotta get cracking. You mind?" She turned to Granny, winked, and mouthed, "*It's cool.*" Then she ran up the stairs.

I think Granny was still going to level with the mayor about no silverware, but Mr. Budd barged in. "This coffee tastes like mule pudding," he said, scribbling on his notepad. "Next time, I'm bringing my own tea bags. What kind of a joint are you running here?"

Granny's jaw dropped. The mayor looked like somebody had thrown mule pudding on his suit. Only Mr. Roosevelt came to the rescue. "Alexander Roosevelt," he said in his most dashing accent. He shook the mayor's hand.

"May I say that I have traveled widely and never happened upon a more delightful village than your fair town."

The corners of the mayor's lips began to turn upward. "Well, I …"

"And what you—and your handsome son— are doing to help the nation's less fortunate! Why, I only hope someone somewhere has the decency to give you the award you deserve."

I thought the mayor was going to burst his buttons. He chatted with Mr. Roosevelt as if they were old buddies.

"Quentin," I said, joining him at his post by the front doors, "isn't Mr. Roosevelt great?"

Quentin nodded but seemed lost in his watch, preparing for countdown. "Dirt has three minutes," he said.

Granny, the librarian, Sunny, and I put the last of the food on the table—fettuccine, salad, cake—not exactly finger food.

Haley didn't seem worried at all. "Mr. Roosevelt said he met a princess once and I reminded him of her." She giggled.

Quentin took his position at the door. Still no Dirt. I couldn't believe Dirt would let us down. The mayor was staring at one of the tables now, probably noticing there was nothing to eat with.

Quentin started: "10-9-8-7-6-5-4-3-2-1—Open!"

Mr. Roosevelt swung the door open. The first one inside was Dirt. She ran in and dumped a paper sack out onto the table.

"Chopsticks?" I asked, as I stared at the pile on the table.

"Mr. Chan and I go way back," Dirt explained.

It was like a Chinese party that night in Granny's church. Everybody laughed as they tried to get the hang of eating noodles, salad, and cake with chopsticks. Dirt was great at it. She must have given a zillion lessons. Even the mayor thought it was a fun idea, though he and Trevor didn't stay.

"Mae," the mayor said, "I'll look forward to Saturday." He and Trevor started to go.

"I'm leaving too," Ben said, starting up the stairs after him.

"Molly," Sunny called. "Don't let Ben leave."

I ran over to Sunny.

"His pockets," she said. "He's got something in his pockets."

"Ben, wait," I said.

Ben turned around, halfway up the stairs. Sunny and I climbed up to meet him. I didn't want anyone else in the dining room to hear what was going on. Trevor and his dad were already out the door. It was just Sunny, Ben, and me. And Ben had us outweighed.

"What's the matter with you, Mack?" he growled. I hate being called *Mack,* and he knows it.

I pointed to his bulging pockets. We had him red-handed this time. "How could you steal Granny's silverware, Ben?" I asked.

"Are you crazier than I thought you were, Mack?" Ben asked. He turned and started up the steps.

I charged up after him, my heart racing so fast my head felt like drums. I made a grab for his coat pocket, stuck in my hand, and pulled out something. "Oh yeah?" I said. "Then what do you call this, Ben Benson?"

Ben looked at me like I had spaghetti all over me. "A cheese stick."

"It *is* a cheese stick," I said stupidly.

"Hey, you're not as dumb as you look, Mack," Ben said. "And this is a cookie." He pulled one thing after another out of his pockets. "This is a roll. Here. Can you say *drumstick?*"

That's all Ben had. No silverware. He left,

cackling. Sunny said Ben still might have done it. But I wasn't so sure. His pockets weren't bulging the night before. The Vulture clubhouse was clean. So where was the missing silverware?

When the meal was over, in walked the delivery boy with a box of silverware. Granny laughed out loud and gave the boy a hug.

Sunny and I washed the silverware and put it away. When we finished, Sunny picked up the towel and peered under it. She bent down and felt around the floor. "Molly, have you seen my watch?" Sunny asked. "I took it off to do dishes."

Granny Mae joined us. "That's funny," she said. "I've been looking all over for *my* watch."

We searched the kitchen and moved to the dining room.

"Excuse me," said a soft voice. I recognized the woman. She had come through the serving line. She looked about Granny Mae's age, with gray hair and wrinkles that spread like little fans at the corners of her eyes. "I was wondering if you could help me. I seem to have lost my watch."

Granny Mae looked to me with wide eyes that said what I was already thinking: *First silverware. Now watches!*

8

New Clue,
For You!

The next morning when I came down to breakfast, Chuckie, my little brother, was squishing bananas between his fingers.

"Chuckie, no," Mom cried. "In the cereal bowl." Mom still wore her fuzzy robe. She didn't look much like a university professor. "Molly," she said, picking up banana from the floor, "I found that on the step this morning."

Without looking, she pointed to the kitchen table. "Do you have a secret admirer? Maybe it's an early valentine, Molly."

On the table was a scroll, a crinkly, parchment-like, rolled-up note. "It's like the one Granny got," I said.

"That's nice," Mom said, making a dive for Chuckie's juice glass as it tipped. "Your dad and I might drop in and help out. I think it's a great idea to—*Chuckie!*"

I didn't look up to see what Chuckie had done this time. I picked up the scroll and untied the string. Slowly, I unrolled it and tried to flatten it on the table. But I couldn't read it. It said:

Dir ti slik each imneys weep
sole the rha veab room.

Andi fac luey ou're look in gfor
you'll fin di tinth isroom.

Ha le yisth epr et tyone
sos he cans erv eth ed rink.

Bu tk now thec lue yo u're loo king for
wil lnot bew hat yout hink.

I had to call a special meeting of the Cinnamon Lakers immediately. Dirt answered her phone. She said she'd get Haley to the bus stop in 30 minutes, even if she had to drag her there. I expected Quentin to put up a fight or come up with a different—better—idea. But he said he'd be right there. He wanted to examine the envelope himself.

51

"Terrific!" Sunny said when I'd filled her in on the phone. "And I've always wanted to ride a school bus. Let me ask my father." I could hear Sunny's side of the conversation. I don't think her dad was as excited about the idea as Sunny was. "But Father," she said, "the other kids take Mr. Winkle's bus every morning. He can't be that bad a driver."

Sunny's dad must have seen Mr. Winkle behind the wheel. It took some begging. But after a minute, Sunny came back on the line. "I'll be there!"

Dad agreed to drop me off at the bus stop on his way out of Cinnamon Lake. I carried my stocking cap. I was trying a new hairdo … for Trevor. I wanted him to notice me. I'd already bought him a valentine. It was worth frozen ears to look more sophisticated. Beauty costs.

Dad's car was so cold, I couldn't get my door open. Overhead, geese honked. A woodpecker thumped a beat on a tree somewhere.

Dad yanked his door, got in, and banged mine from the inside. "Next summer, I'm building a garage," Dad said. He says that every February.

Halfway there, Dad pulled a small card out of his pocket. "Molly, what do you think of my new business card? Just a sideline, you understand."

He shoved one at me. It read: *What's in a name? Everything. Get more for your message!*

Below it said, *Mack's Messages*.

"I like it," I said. And there's no letter missing, I thought.

Quentin was already at the bus stop, waiting for me to turn over the note. His down jacket and mittens made him look plumper. He pulled off one mitten and ran his fingers over the parchment. He took out a magnifying glass and studied the letters.

"Um-hmm," he mumbled. "Like Granny's. It has been wet, soaked in a substance yet to be identified. That's what gives it the old, parchment effect." He unrolled it and studied the coded message in silence.

Dirt was as good as her word. She came running up the lane, dragging her sister behind her.

A big black limousine drove up and Sunny hopped out. "No. I'll be fine, Father. The bus will be a great experience."

We huddled around the bus bench.

"Is that a donut?" Quentin asked Haley. "A chocolate donut?"

For an answer, Haley popped the rest into her mouth.

Quentin looked like he'd lost his best friend. "Mother is on her natural food kick once more. I had Grape-Nuts for breakfast. No sugar. No grape. No nuts. No taste. Was that donut frosted, Haley?"

"Yes. And so am I," Haley whined. "I can't

believe you'd call a Cinnamon Laker meeting in the middle of the night, Molly!"

"Haley," I said, "it's hardly the middle of the night. We got another note. Quentin's working on it now."

"No," Quentin said, eyeing the chocolate crumbs on Haley's chin. "I cracked it."

"You did?" I asked, once again amazed at Quentin's gray cells. "What's it say?"

Dirt, Sunny, and I crowded around the note. Quentin had drawn lines between letters, regrouping them:

Dir t/i s/lik e/a/ch imney/s weep/
so/le t/he r/ha ve/a/b room.

And/i f/a/c lue/y ou're/ look in g/for/
y ou'll/ fin d/i t/in/th is/room.

Ha le y/is/th e/pr et ty/one/
so/s he/ can/s erv e/th e/d rink.

Bu t/k now/ the/c lue/ yo u're/ loo king/
for/wil l/not/ be/w hat/ you/t hink.

I read the new words: "Dirt is like a chimney sweep, so let her have a broom. And if a clue you're

54

looking for, you'll find it in this room. Haley is the pretty one, so she can serve the drink. But know the clue you're looking for will not be what you think."

"Far out," Dirt said. "A chimney sweep. I like it."

"The rhyme and meter show a certain level of education," Quentin said.

"They're clues to something," I said.

"Brilliant, Sherlock," Haley said. "Anybody might have written that part about me being the pretty one."

"I mean, it's like we'll find something if we follow the clues. Maybe we'll find the watches. Maybe even the silverware," I said.

"Wouldn't that be great!" Sunny squealed. "Then Granny could get her money back. She could put on a Valentine's dinner good enough for the mayor. My father said most of the businesspeople in Cinnamon don't like the idea of a soup kitchen. They're afraid it might bring in the wrong kind of people."

"Like that Budd character," Haley said, making a face. She seemed to notice me for the first time that morning. "Molly," she asked, "what happened to your hair?"

"Never mind," I said. I pulled on my stocking cap.

"Fifth grade alert!" Dirt hollered. Several students had straggled into the bus stop. We all huddled together in a circle, like it was a tornado drill. Marty and Ben were coming.

"Here comes the bus!" Sunny sounded as though Mr. Winkle were leading the grand parade.

Ben said, "Well, if it isn't the little rich girl. Are you slumming, Sunny? Isn't Daddy taking you to school?"

"Buzz off, Ben," Dirt said.

Mr. Winkle came so close to our bench, we backed up fast. We piled on the bus.

Sam Benson ran up just as Mr. Winkle was closing the bus doors. "Ben didn't wake me," he said, panting. Sam plopped down across from Dirt and me and glared at Ben. "So now what are you guys going to do with yourselves?" he asked.

"What do you mean?" I asked.

"Now that there's no more soup kitchen." He took off his gloves and blew on his fingers.

"Sam, what are you talking about? We're going to Granny's church after school. She still has her soup kitchen."

"You mean you didn't hear?" Sam looked from me to Dirt and back again. "I'm not kidding, Molly. Granny called Marty's mom this morning. Cross my heart. Granny Mae's soup kitchen has been canceled."

9

Measure, Sift
Rhyming Gift

The Cinnamon Lakers agreed to go straight to Granny's church after school like we'd planned. As we hopped off the quiet bus in front of the church, I still didn't know if Sam was lying or not. Granny wouldn't close the soup kitchen.

At first, I thought the church was empty. No songs. No laughter. "Granny Mae? Are you here?" I hollered down the stairs.

"Yes, I'm here," she called. Her voice echoed. She was sitting all alone at one of the long metal tables. "I'm sorry," she said. "I called you this morning to tell you not to come. But you had already left for school."

"Granny?" Quentin put his hand on his grandmother's shoulder. "You really canceled your soup kitchen?"

Her eyes looked red. "I had to," she said.

"But what are you going to do when they show up for supper?" I asked. "And your Valentine's dinner tomorrow night? What about the mayor and everybody?"

"There's nothing to feed them, girl." Granny waved her arm toward the kitchen. "Word got out we were robbed. By the time I went to bed last night, six businesses called to say they wouldn't be sending any more food our way. Now how am I going to get around that? I wanted to help these folks. Instead, they came here and got what little they had stolen. I've been sitting here praying about it, but I haven't got a clue."

"We got clues." Dirt shoved her way between Granny and Quentin. "We got clues."

"Dirt's right," I said. "Somebody left us clues. We think they might lead to the stolen silverware and watches." I'd been going over the first part of the note all day in my head. "I think I've figured out part of it. *Dirt is like a chimney sweep, so let her have a broom. And if a clue you're looking for, you'll find it in this room.* Get it? The room with a broom."

Then it was Sunny's turn. "*Haley is the pret-*

ty one, so she can serve the drink. But know the clue you're looking for will not be what you think. Like there's a clue where you serve the drinks." She ran to the serving cart and looked under it. She came up empty. "Or maybe it's where you store the drinks."

"Cups," Dirt said. Dirt dashed to the closet where Granny stored the broom and my dad's misspelled paper cups.

We searched the closet and turned up everything from crepe paper to crayons and old church bulletins. But no silverware. And no watches.

"How 'bout this?" Dirt asked. She crawled out from behind a stack of newspapers. Under her arm was a greenish shoe box with a rubber band around it. "Smells funny," she said. "Like peppermint, but that's not it."

Quentin shook the box. "It isn't heavy enough to be silverware or watches," he said, his voice sinking. "I'm beginning to think this note is nothing more than a cruel hoax."

Dirt handed the box to Granny Mae.

"Wonder what this is," Granny said. "I don't remember seeing it in here last night." She slid off the rubber band and lifted the lid. "Mercy!" She gasped and shut the lid.

"What is it, Granny Mae?" I asked.

Her mouth opened and closed, but no words came out. If her eyes had gotten any wider, her face would have disappeared.

Quentin took the shoe box out of Granny Mae's arms. Her arms stayed in midair, frozen, as if she still held the box.

"Once again it falls to me to investigate," Quentin said. He pulled off the lid. Quentin's face looked like a copy of Granny Mae's. Then he dropped the box as if it burned his fingers.

My gasp mixed with everyone else's. The shoe box turned over in the air. Out of it flew the most money I had ever seen in my whole life!

10

Soup's On
All Gone

"It's a miracle!" Granny Mae said at last. "Lord, we thank You. And I'm sorry I ever doubted Your calling."

We picked up the bills that lay all over the closet. Quentin estimated about $200. I started to put a handful of ten-dollar bills into the shoe box when I noticed a piece of wrinkly paper taped to the bottom of the box. It looked like parchment. I pulled it off. "Now that's weird," I said, turning the paper over and back. "There's nothing written on this one."

Dirt snatched it from me and sniffed. "Not mint. Same, but different. And lemon."

"You make about as much sense as these clues, Dirt," Quentin said. He took the new clue and ran his finger over it. "Something has been written here."

"Invisible ink?" Sunny asked.

"I shall need my laboratory before I answer." Quentin tucked the note into his pocket.

Granny stood straight, with her eyes closed. I knew she was praying. She opened her eyes and winked at me. "I've been so wrapped up in how dark things appeared for my soup kitchen, I forgot things are not always what they appear."

"What do you mean, Granny?" I asked.

"When Jesus died on that cross, I imagine His followers thought things couldn't get darker. They got so blinded by that darkness, they almost missed the light when Jesus rose from the dead. No, sir, things are not always as they appear. Granny Mae's soup kitchen is still in business."

Bang! Somebody kicked the closet door. "Mowry! Come out."

"Chuckie?" I said. I opened the door a crack and peeked out. Chuckie stood there with his hands on his hips and something blue all over his mouth. "What are you doing here?"

"There you are," Dad said, coming up behind my brother. "Where is everybody, Molly? It's almost five. Can you come help your mom in the kitchen?"

I followed Dad. I glanced back at the closet to see Granny Mae, Sunny, Dirt, and Haley sneaking out.

In the kitchen, Mom stood over a huge, silver pot. She was giving orders to Mr. Roosevelt and Mr. Budd. "Two more sacks in the trunk," she told Mr. Budd. "Hi, honey," she said when she spotted me. "There you are, Mae. I couldn't reach you. Is this a good night? I didn't know what you were serving. Don't you start at five? Or aren't you serving tonight?"

"We are now," Granny said. "What did you bring?"

Mom grinned. "Soup, of course."

"Cool," Dirt said. "Now we've got us a real soup kitchen."

Even without the other helpers, we were only a few minutes late opening the soup kitchen doors. There wasn't as much food as usual, but nobody complained. Nobody except Mr. Budd. He stormed around sipping his tea. He'd had to bring his own tea bags. Then there was no lemon to put in his tea. And then we didn't have Tabasco sauce, and he said Mom's soup needed it. Mr. Roosevelt, on the other hand, glided around the kitchen, filling in for everybody.

"I don't think it's a mystery who left that money," Haley said. "It had to be Mr. Roosevelt.

I'll bet he's a millionaire who travels around spending his money."

The thought had entered my mind. Mr. Roosevelt showed up at the same time Granny got her note. His clothes were nicer than anybody's in that church, except Sunny's. And he sure seemed like a high-class gentleman.

"That's not all," Haley went on. "I know who the thief is too. Mr. Budd the Complainer. Can you believe the way he whines?"

I bit my tongue. I wasn't sure who would win a whining contest—Haley or Mr. Budd. Still, if the Vultures weren't guilty, that did kind of leave Mr. Budd. But we'd have to get some real evidence before we could accuse him.

The rest of the night I kept my eye on Mr. Budd. Quentin didn't reappear until we were cleaning up dishes. He had his coat and stocking cap on. I hoped he'd found a safe place for Granny's shoe box money. She'd need every dollar to pull off her Valentine's dinner in less than 24 hours. "Where is it?" I whispered.

Quentin raised his eyebrows, glanced both ways, then patted his stocking cap. That was why it looked so fat! He had the money under his hat.

After everybody else left, Dad and I finished up the dishes. Mom and Granny Mae mopped

"Quentin, not another closet."

He ignored me. He pulled a string, and a lightbulb that hung from the ceiling clicked on. "It took several tests before I determined the note had been written in citrus."

"Citrus?" I asked, imagining a foreign language. From the country of Sit.

"Lemon juice, to be precise, though I believe orange or grapefruit would have served as well. Watch this." He held the paper to the light. It had black marks on it. But as the paper warmed under the light, I saw deeper black marks appear.

"As you may or may not know," Quentin continued, "citrus is a carbon-based substance, a combination of carbon and other elements. Therefore, as one heats the substance, the elements separate. You are witnessing the carbon in the form of black—now visible—ink."

He brought the paper down. Figures, like Chinese writing, were clearly there:

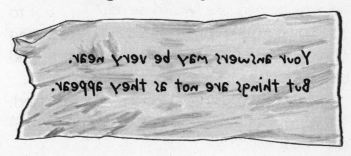

"So what's it say?" I asked, feeling that the answer was in my hands.

"You have to hold it to a mirror."

I knew the basement bathroom had a mirror. I ran down the stairs, past the kitchen, to the bathroom. Dirt broke away from whomever she'd been talking to in the kitchen and ran after me. I let her in and closed the door. She watched as I held the paper up to the mirror and read:

> *Your answers may be very near.*
> *But things are not as they appear.*

"That's no clue," I said. "What good is that?"

Dirt took the note and sniffed. She frowned at the paper and left.

"It's about time," Mr. Budd said when we joined the others in the kitchen. He dipped a tea bag in one of Dad's cups. "Kids."

"What a grouch," Haley said. "Why can't he be a gentleman, like Mr. Roosevelt?"

I frowned after Mr. Budd. Granny Mae leaned down and whispered, "Be nice to Mr. Budd. He's not as tough as he appears."

"Why, will you look at this lovely lady!" called Mr. Roosevelt. He was peering up through the basement window.

Dirt, Haley, and I went over to check it out. At the base of a bush, a bright, red cardinal pecked at something on the ground. "That's no lady," Dirt said.

"No?" said Mr. Roosevelt. "But the bright allure, the beauty and charm, surely …"

"Nope," Dirt said. "In the bird world, boys are brightly colored. Girl cardinals are gray."

Things are not as they appear. The mystery note popped into my mind.

We covered the table with red paper Granny had bought with extra shoe box money. She and the librarian hung hearts all over the basement. With the rest of the money, Granny got stuff to cook a meal fit for kings. Good thing because the closest thing Cinnamon had to royalty would be showing up. And everything had to be perfect.

Fifteen minutes before the doors would open, Quentin called the Cinnamon Lakers together in one corner. "It is of the utmost importance that nothing be stolen this evening. The mayor, businesspeople, and most of the town council will be here. If a crime occurs tonight, that will be the end of Granny Mae's soup kitchen. So be watchful."

"And keep your eyes on Mr. Budd," Haley said.

"We don't know he did it," I said.

"Just look at him," Haley said. "Then tell me he's not the most likely suspect."

"Cinnamon Lakers," Granny called.

Poor Granny Mae. I felt like we'd let her down. She'd hired us to find out before tonight who sent her the note. We'd failed. We hadn't solved *that* mystery or the next. Now her whole mission was in trouble. I said a quick prayer and asked that everything would come out okay.

When the doors opened, we stood to greet the guests. The crowd parted to let Trevor and his dad go in first. Then followed store owners, the town council, teachers, everybody.

"Hey, Molly."

I turned to see Trevor's big blue eyes. He motioned with his head for me to come over. My face burned, and I knew I had to be blushing, matching the valentine I clutched in the apron Granny had tied on me. Maybe Trevor had a valentine for me too.

"Hi, Trevor," I said. "Happy Valentine's Day." I started to take out the valentine.

"Is she Chinese or what?" he asked. He nodded in Sunny's direction.

For a minute, I didn't know if I'd heard him right. "Do you mean Sunny?" I asked.

Trevor laughed, a making-fun-of laugh. "Is she making chop suey for everybody?"

I smiled, wanting to laugh with him. This was the most Trevor had ever said to me. But something didn't feel right about it. I didn't answer him.

"Why do you hang out with the Cinnamon Lakers, Molly?" he asked. "What are you, like multicolored or something? You and Haley ought to hook up with the Vultures."

In my pocket, I squeezed Trevor's valentine into a ball of trash. "Sunny *and* Quentin are two of my best friends, Trevor," I said. "And I'm proud to be a Cinnamon Laker with them."

I turned my back on Trevor and joined my friends. I'd finally met the real Trevor. *Things are not as they appear,* I thought.

Granny Mae's Valentine's dinner went better than we'd imagined. At one table sat the sheriff, his deputy, the mayor, and most of the town's business leaders. And in the middle of them, right next to the mayor, sat Mr. Roosevelt, charming them with stories and questions. Every now and then a burst of laughter erupted from that table as Mr. Roosevelt finished another tale.

Granny Mae beamed as she flitted from table to table, telling everyone to thank God, not her.

"Molly," she said when the last dessert had been served, "what more could we ask for?"

A tinkling on a water glass stopped my answer. The mayor tapped his glass with a spoon until the room got quiet. "Ladies and gentlemen," he said, getting to his feet, "if I may have your attention. I would like to thank Granny Mae and her soup kitchen for a delightful Valentine's feast. It's a fine and worthy thing you're doing for these poor people."

Granny glanced uncomfortably around the room. I knew she didn't like us to call our guests "poor people."

"To show my appreciation," the mayor continued, "I'd like to be the first to give my donation to this good work." He reached into his pocket and looked at the other people at his table. "I'd like all of you to dig deep to help the poor today," he said.

The mayor dug deep into one pocket. With a puzzled look on his face, he dug into the other pocket. He patted his shirt. Sounding embarrassed, he said, "I ... I ... seemed to have misplaced my wallet."

He'd just gotten the words out, when the man across the table from him yelled, "Hey, my wallet's gone."

Then the sheriff stood up. "My wallet's gone too. Somebody stole my wallet!"

And one by one, almost everybody at that table hollered out the same thing. Somebody had stolen all the wallets in Granny Mae's Valentine's soup kitchen!

12

What's in a Name?
The End of the Game

"Nobody move," said the sheriff. "One of you is a thief." He turned to Mr. Budd, who was sitting quietly at the end of the table. "You," he said, "you've been hanging around here a lot lately."

"Search him, Sheriff," said the mayor.

Mr. Budd didn't say a word. He slowly lifted his eyes, and I thought for sure he was looking right at me. The mystery note ran through my mind. *Things are not as they appear.*

"Wait a minute," I said.

"Yes," Granny Mae said. "Just a minute here."

But nobody paid any attention to us. The sheriff and his deputy moved to Mr. Budd's chair and looked down at him.

"Perhaps a search might settle the matter," suggested Mr. Roosevelt. He leaned back in his chair, his arms folded across his chest.

"Good idea," said the mayor. "Search him."

Mr. Budd didn't fight. The deputy searched one pocket and came out empty. Then the sheriff stuck his hand into the other pocket. He came out with a gold stopwatch.

"That's my stopwatch!" screamed the mayor. "That thief stole my stopwatch. Arrest that man, Sheriff!"

"What's your name?" asked the sheriff, pulling Mr. Budd to his feet.

"Budd," he answered.

"*I* knew all along he was the thief," Haley said. "Budd. It's probably not even his real name."

"Ah, yes," Mr. Roosevelt said, shaking his head. "And what's in a name? Everything."

"Right you are," said the mayor.

What's in a name? Everything. Where had I heard that before? Something was playing hide-and-seek in my mind. Then I got it. Dad's business card! But how did Mr. Roosevelt …

"Hold everything!" I cried so loudly that everyone turned toward me. "Let him go."

"He's committed a crime," said the mayor. "Anybody can see that."

"Things are not as they appear," I said. "You've got the wrong man."

I turned to Mr. Roosevelt. "Mr. Roosevelt, that quote you just said about names, *What's in a name? Everything.* I know where you got it."

"What's this little girl talking about?" asked the mayor. "Who cares where it came from?"

"It came from my dad's new business cards. He had them in his wallet last night when *somebody* stole *his* wallet. Mr. Roosevelt, I think that somebody was you." I didn't know if anybody would believe me. "Would you let the sheriff search you?"

"I am hurt and disappointed in your lack of trust in me, Molly. I thought we were friends," said Mr. Roosevelt.

"Me too, sir," I said.

"Well, what about it, Roosevelt?" said the sheriff. "Want to put her mind at ease?" He didn't let go of Mr. Budd. But he nodded to the deputy to search Mr. Roosevelt.

"Now, just one moment," Mr. Roosevelt said, slowly pushing his chair back. Then suddenly he made a run for it.

"Stop!" yelled the sheriff. But Mr. Roosevelt was almost to the stairs.

Then Mr. Roosevelt screamed and flew off his feet, smack on the floor. "*Yaieee!*" His coat flew up. Wallets and watches dropped out everywhere.

Dirt stepped from the stairwell. She had tripped Mr. Roosevelt by sticking out her foot at exactly the right moment. She stood over him as the sheriff and deputy put handcuffs on him. "Cool," she said.

"Into every life some rain must fall," said Mr. Roosevelt as they led him away.

"That's it!" said the deputy. "Now I know where I've seen this guy before. His picture is on a wanted poster in the sheriff's office. It's on your bulletin board, Sheriff. The Gentleman Pickpocket! He's got a rap sheet a mile long."

The sheriff squinted at Mr. Roosevelt. "*You're* the Gentleman Pickpocket?"

"I repeat," said Mr. Roosevelt, without a trace of accent now, "what's in a name? Everything."

Turns out Mr. Roosevelt had been charming his way across three states. Mr. Budd handed back the mayor's stopwatch. Mr. Roosevelt had slipped it into Mr. Budd's pocket to make him look guilty. The rest of Granny's stuff was in Mr. Roosevelt's backpack. We watched them lead away the Gentleman Pickpocket.

"Well, if Mr. Roosevelt didn't give Granny money," Haley asked, "who did?"

"Earl Grey," Dirt said.

"Who's that?" whined Haley.

"Not who," Dirt explained. "*What.* Earl Grey is a kind of tea. I smelled peppermint tea on the first note. The last note was lemon and something I couldn't get. Then I remembered. Earl Grey."

Dirt learned all about herbs and teas from Mrs. Crocker, an old woman who lives at Cinnamon Lake. We used to call her "Off-Her-Rocker Crocker" until we got to know her. She and Dirt grow herbs in the middle of the woods.

"Tea!" Quentin said. "That explains the parchment look of the notes. They were soaked in water with tea bags to make them look old and brown."

Lemon. Tea. A picture flashed through my gray cells. Mr. Budd complaining about no tea. Then another picture of Mr. Budd, his own tea bags in hand, complaining because we didn't have any lemon.

"Mr. Budd?" I asked, almost in a whisper. "*You're* the mystery millionaire?" It all fits now. If we hadn't been judging books by their covers, and people by their clothes, we would have figured it out before. But his clothes! How could he give money away?

Granny Mae ran up and gave Mr. Budd a hug. "You're living off social security like I am," she said. "How could you afford to give all that money?"

"I had some savings put away," Mr. Budd said, not looking up from the table. "I just came here to make sure it was used right." Then so soft I almost missed it, he mumbled, "It was."

"You sure were right, Mr. Budd," I said. "Our answers *were* very near. And things were not as they appeared."

I breathed a sigh of relief that all mysteries were solved and cases closed. I leaned against the wall and stuck my hands in my pockets. That's when I felt the valentine I'd bought for Trevor. When I pulled it out, it felt pretty wrinkled, like the parchment. "Happy Valentine's Day, Mr. Budd," I said, handing him the crumpled heart.

Mr. Budd looked up and almost smiled. "Yeah," he said, "I guess it is at that."

Help the Cinnamon Lakers solve these mysteries too!

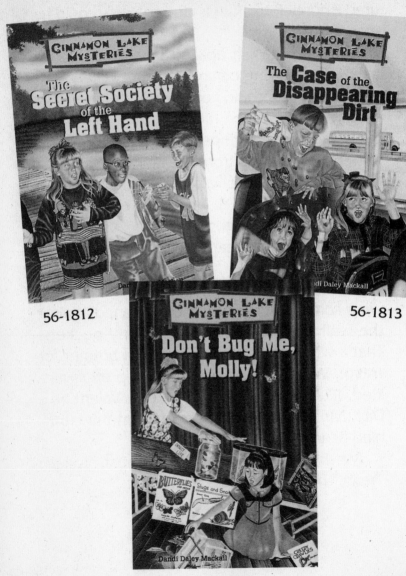

56-1812

56-1813

56-1833